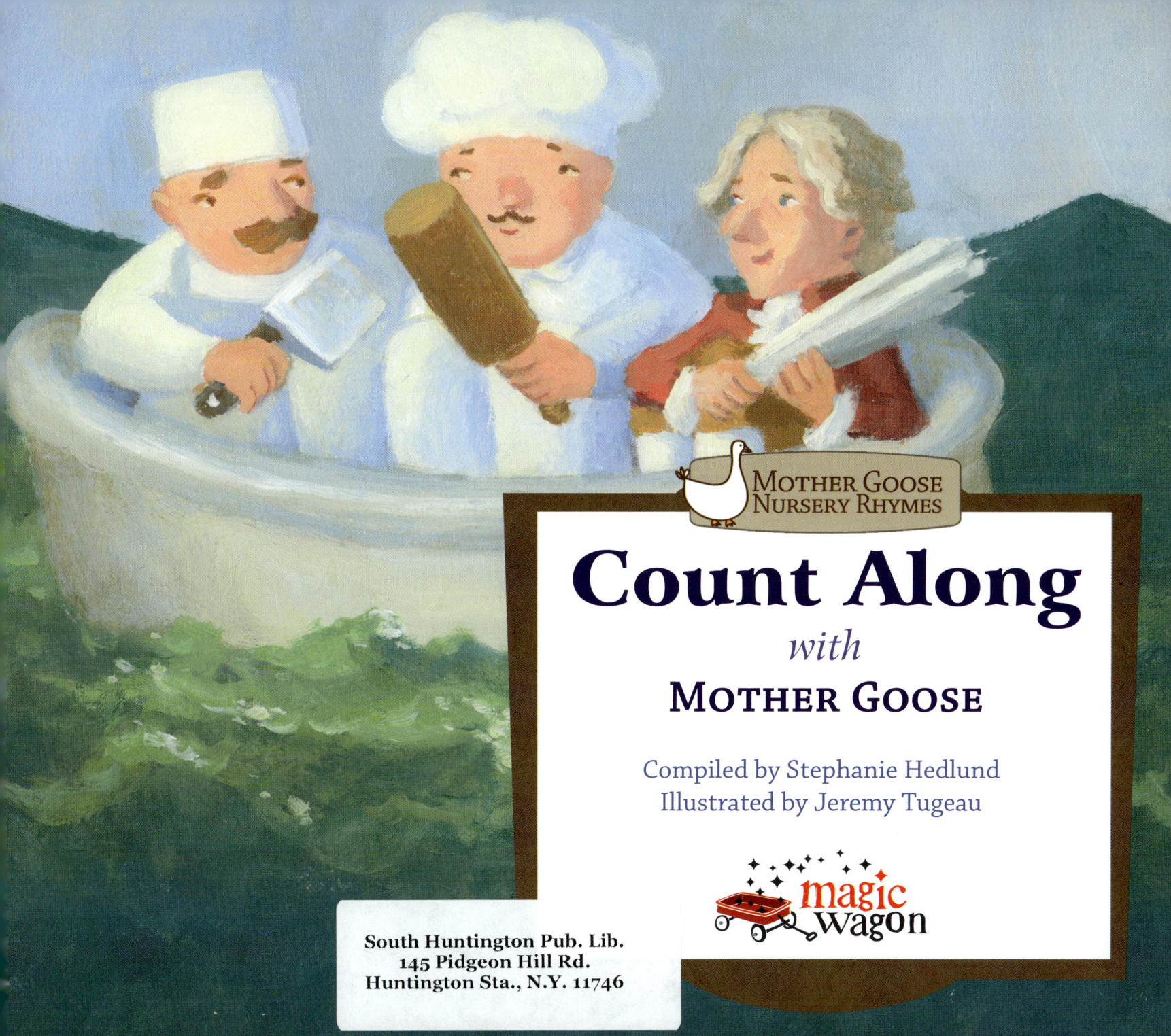

visit us at www.abdopublishing.com

Published by Magic Wagon, a division of the ABDO Group, 8000 West 78th Street, Edina, Minnesota 55439. Copyright © 2011 by Abdo Consulting Group, Inc. International copyrights reserved in all countries. All rights reserved. No part of this book may be reproduced in any form without written permission from the publisher.

Looking Glass Library™ is a trademark and logo of Magic Wagon.

Printed in the United States of America, North Mankato, Minnesota.
102010
012011
 This book contains at least 10% recycled materials.

Compiled by Stephanie Hedlund
Illustrations by Jeremy Tugeau
Edited by Rochelle Baltzer
Cover and interior layout and design by Abbey Fitzgerald

Library of Congress Cataloging-in-Publication Data

Count along with Mother Goose / compiled by Stephanie Hedlund ; illustrated by Jeremy Tugeau.
     v. cm. -- (Mother Goose nursery rhymes)
   Contents: Nursery rhymes about counting -- Three times round -- One two, buckle my shoe -- One for the money -- How many chickens? -- Thirty days -- Sing a song of sixpence -- Hot cross buns! -- Gregory Griggs -- I saw three ships -- Old King Cole -- Rub-a-dub-dub -- Hickory, dickory, dock -- Three young rats.
  ISBN 978-1-61641-144-2
 1. Nursery rhymes. 2. Children's poetry. [1. Nursery rhymes. 2. Counting.]
 I. Hedlund, Stephanie F., 1977- II. Tugeau, Jeremy, ill. III. Mother Goose.
  PZ8.3.C8293 2011
  398.8 [E]--dc22
                    2010024696

Contents

Nursery Rhymes About Counting 4
Three Times Round 6
One, Two, Buckle My Shoe 8
One for the Money 10
How Many Chickens? 12
Thirty Days 14
Sing a Song of Sixpence 16
Hot Cross Buns! 18
Gregory Griggs 20
I Saw Three Ships 22
Old King Cole 24
Rub-a-Dub-Dub 26
Hickory, Dickory, Dock 28
Three Young Rats 30
Glossary 32
Web Sites 32

Nursery Rhymes
About Counting

Since early days, people have created rhymes to teach and entertain children. Since they were often said in a nursery, they became known as nursery rhymes. In the 1700s, these nursery rhymes were collected and published to share with parents and other adults.

Some of these collections were named after Mother Goose. Mother Goose didn't actually exist, but there are many stories about who she could be. Her rhymes were so popular, people began using *Mother Goose rhymes* to refer to most nursery rhymes.

Since the 1600s, nursery rhymes have come from many sources. The meanings of the rhymes have been lost, but they are an important form of folk language. Nursery rhymes about animals have long been used to teach children to count. Animals, people, and things are all included in these teaching rhymes.

Three times round goes our gallant ship,
And three times round goes she,
Three times round goes our gallant ship,
And sinks to the bottom of the sea.

One, two, buckle my shoe;
Three, four, open the door;
Five, six, pick up sticks;
Seven, eight, lay them straight;
Nine, ten, a big fat hen;
Eleven, twelve, I hope you're well;
Thirteen, fourteen, draw the curtain;
Fifteen, sixteen, the maid's in the kitchen;
Seventeen, eighteen, she's in waiting;
Nineteen, twenty, my stomach's empty
Please, ma'am, to give me some dinner.

One for the Money

One for the money,
And two for the show,
Three to make ready,
And four to go.

Chook, chook, chook, chook, chook,
Good morning, Mrs. Hen.
How many chickens have you got?
Madam, I've got ten.
Four of them are yellow,
And four of them are brown,
And two of them are speckled red,
The nicest in the town.

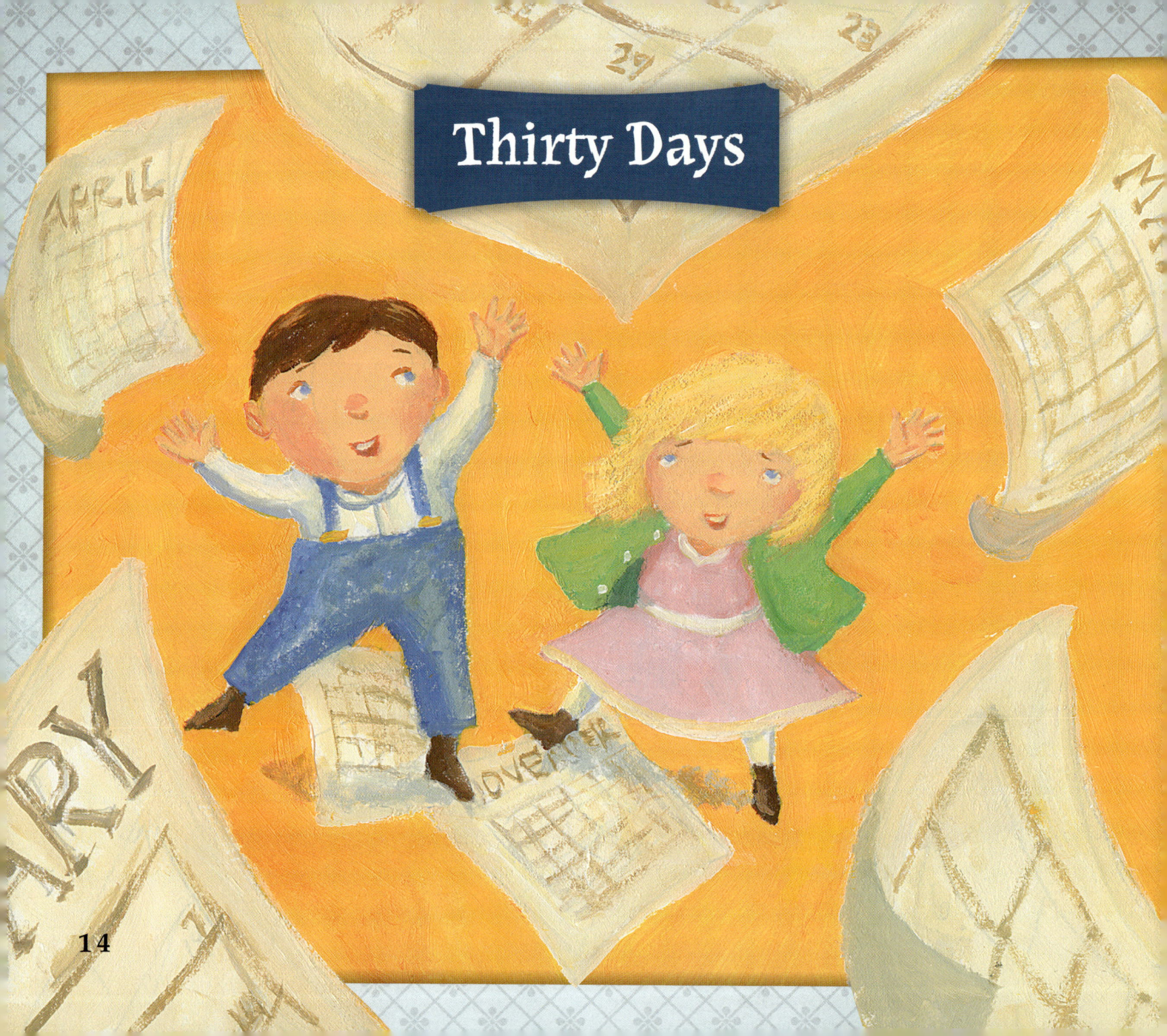

Thirty days hath September,
April, June, and November;
All the rest have thirty-one,
Excepting February alone,
And that has twenty-eight days clear
And twenty-nine in each leap year.

Sing a song of sixpence,
A pocket full of rye;
Four and twenty blackbirds
Baked in a pie.

When the pie was opened
The birds began to sing;
Was not that a dainty dish
To set before the king?

The king was in his counting house
Counting out his money;
The queen was in the parlor
Eating bread and honey.

The maid was in the garden
Hanging out the clothes;
There came a little blackbird,
And snapped off her nose.

Hot cross buns!

Hot cross buns!

One a penny, two a penny,

Hot cross buns!

If your daughters do not like them,

Give them to your sons;

But if you haven't any of these pretty little elves,

You cannot do better than eat them yourselves.

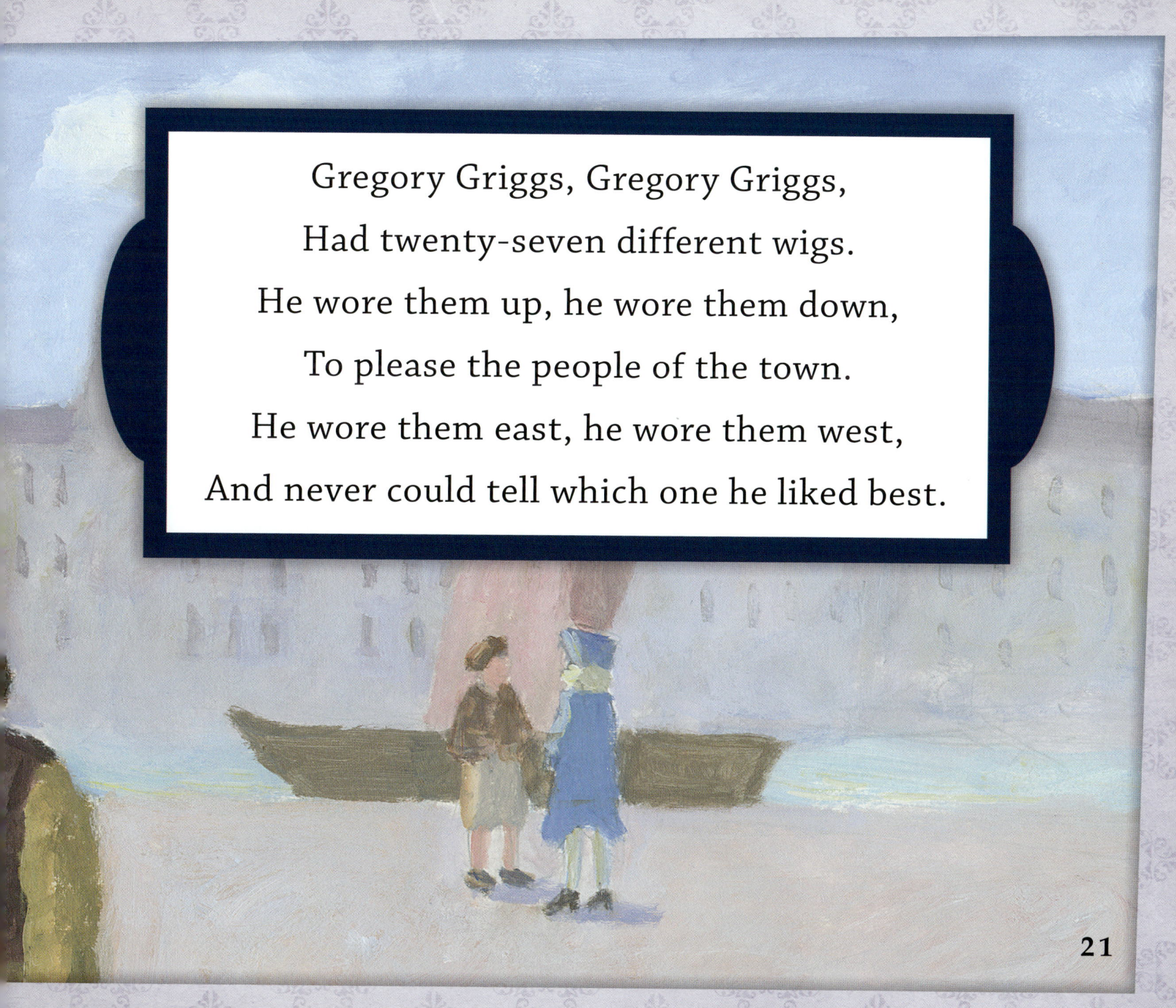

Gregory Griggs, Gregory Griggs,
Had twenty-seven different wigs.
He wore them up, he wore them down,
To please the people of the town.
He wore them east, he wore them west,
And never could tell which one he liked best.

I saw three ships come sailing by,
Come sailing by, come sailing by,
I saw three ships come sailing by,
On New Year's Day in the morning.

And what do you think was in them then,
Was in them then, was in them then?
And what do you think was in them then?
On New Year's Day in the morning?

Three pretty girls were in them then,
Were in them then, were in them then,
Three pretty girls were in them then,
On New Year's Day in the morning.

One could whistle, and one could sing,
And one could play the violin;
Such joy was there at my wedding,
On New Year's Day in the morning.

Old King Cole
Was a merry old soul,
And a merry old soul was he;
He called for his pipe,
And he called for his bowl,
And he called for his fiddlers three.

Every fiddler, he had a fiddle,
And a very fine fiddle had he;
Twee tweedle dee, tweedle dee, went the fiddlers.
Oh, there's none so rare
As can compare
With King Cole and his fiddlers three.

Rub-a-dub-dub,

Three men in a tub,

And how do you think they got there?

The butcher, the baker,

The candlestick-maker,

They all jumped out of a rotten potato,

'Twas enough to make a man stare.

Hickory, Dickory, Dock

Hickory, dickory, dock,
The mouse ran up the clock.
The clock struck one,
Down the mouse did run.
Hickory, dickory, dock.

Three young rats with black felt hats,
Three young ducks with white straw flats,

Three young dogs with curling tails,
Three young cats with demi-veils,

Went out to walk with two young pigs
In satin vests and sorrel wigs.

But suddenly it chanced to rain
And so they all went home again.

Glossary

dainty – something delicate.

demi-veil – a veil that covers only half of the face.

felt – a cloth made of wool and fur. It is often mixed with other fabrics through the action of heat, moisture, chemicals, and pressure.

gallant – splendid or stately.

hath – an old way of saying *has*.

parlor – a room where guests are entertained.

rye – a type of grain.

sixpence – a British coin that was valued at six pennies.

speckled – to have spots of color.

sorrel – a brownish orange to light brown color.

Web Sites

To learn more about nursery rhymes, visit ABDO Group online at **www.abdopublishing.com**. Web sites about nursery rhymes are featured on our Book Links page. These links are routinely monitored and updated to provide the most current information available.

JAN 1 2 2012
2850